Mulan

Written by Michaela Morgan
Illustrated by Steve Dorado

Long ago and far away, in a land of dragons and battles, there lived a famous warrior. This is the tale of that hero.

Chapter 1

 Mulan was working quietly in her corner of the house, just as she did every day. She was at her loom, weaving, weaving. Just as she did every day.

Shhhhh, shhhhh went the shuttles of her loom.

It was quiet in the house. Mulan's father, tired and ill, was tossing and turning in his bed. Mulan's mother, busy as ever, was making a meal. Little Brother was playing as quietly as Little Brother could.

Shhhhh, shhhhh went the shuttles of the loom. But there was another sound. What was it?

3

It was the sound of Mulan sighing as she worked.
"What is it?" Father asked her.
"Why do you sigh?" Mother asked her.

"Are you dreaming of a boyfriend? Are you wishing for new shoes?" Little Brother asked her. He was a bold boy who liked to tease his older sister.

"I am thinking of the poster I saw in town," said Mulan. She sighed again. "Our country is under attack! We have been ordered to send a man from this family to fight in the emperor's army."

WAR!

One man from every family MUST join the army to fight for the emperor!

 "A man from our family must go to fight or we will all be punished," sighed Mulan's father. "I will do what has to be done."

The sick old man tried to struggle to his feet, but he had no strength to stand.

"You will not last a day!" cried Mulan's mother. "Your fighting days are over."

"I will go instead of Father!" said Little Brother. He picked up his tiny wooden sword and pretended to fight his toys. But he whirled his toy sword so quickly that he lost his footing and fell down.

Mulan looked at her little brother lying in his pile of toys. He was still clutching his toy sword. He was much, much too young to fight for his country.

She looked at her father. He was much, much too old. True, he had once been a very skilled soldier, but those days were long gone.

8

"I am just the right age," she thought. "I can run and ride better than many boys. I can think quickly, and I have helped Father practice his fighting skills for years. I should be the one who joins the army."

Chapter 3

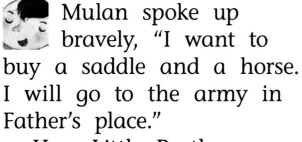 Mulan spoke up bravely, "I want to buy a saddle and a horse. I will go to the army in Father's place."

How Little Brother laughed! "Silly, silly, silly!" he said. "You're only a silly girl."

How Mulan's mother fretted! "No, no, no, it's not right! Your place is here with us. Girls are not allowed in the emperor's army."

Mulan's father was too sick to say much. He just groaned, "No, Mulan, nooo!"

11

Mulan was determined.

"I have a plan," she said. "I will dress like a boy. I'll wear padding and armor. They'll never know I'm a girl!"

"Impossible!" said her mother.

"Dangerous!" gasped her father.

"Crazy!" said Little Brother.

Mulan had made up her mind. She was ready to do anything to save her family.

In the East Market, she got a speedy horse.

In the West Market, she got a saddle.

In the North Market, she got a set of armor.

In the South Market, she got a sword.

Chapter 4

At home she tied up her hair and tried on her armor. All that night she practiced her fighting skills and took tips from her father.

She no longer looked like Mulan. Now she looked like a soldier.

At dawn she said good-bye to her father and mother, climbed onto the back of her speedy horse, and rode away.

"She'll be back by lunch," laughed Little Brother.

Yet Mulan was not back by lunch that day or the next.

Mulan traveled for three days along the banks of the Yellow River. The ground was hard, the air was chilly, and the nights were dark and lonely.

She missed her family, and many times she wished she could go home. But bravely she went on. At dusk on the third day, she arrived at the army camp at Black Mountain.

As Mulan approached the camp, a guard appeared, blocking her way.

"Where are you going?" he challenged. Mulan shivered, but she said in a deep voice, "I am here to join the army as ordered."

The guard nodded. Surprised, Mulan passed quickly into the camp.

From that moment on, Mulan lived in fear of her fellow soldiers discovering she was a girl. Army life was tough. Every day sights and sounds reminded her of home and her family.

The days were long. The nights were longer. The life was harder than hard.

Chapter 5

Mulan didn't give up. She worked hard, and she trained hard. She learned how to use a spear and how to carry a shield. She learned how to attack and defend and how to ride at the speed of the wind.

Soon it was time for the first battle.

Mulan's blood ran cold with dread and fear. Her knees shook. Her heart pounded, but she clutched her sword tightly and went into battle.

Oh, she was as brave as any soldier!
Oh, she was as quick as any runner!

And she was clever! She used her sword, but she also used her brain. She outwitted her enemies.

She used her spear to leap over her attackers. She danced her way past clumsy attacks. She hid under her shield, then jumped out to take her attackers by surprise.

She earned the respect of her fellow soldiers. They still had no idea she was a young girl.

They slapped her on her back and said, "What clever tricks you use!"

That was the first battle of many.

Mulan became a fine warrior. She became a great leader.

She survived one long year, then two years, three years, four, five, six, and seven years more.

For 10 years she fought hard and survived.

She traveled far.
She rode through
large green forests.

She rode across hot
red deserts.
She rode up steep
and snowy mountains.

She rode 1,000 miles,
then 2,000 miles, 3,000,
4,000, 5,000, 6,000, and
7,000 miles more.
During the war she
rode 10,000 miles.

She kept her hair tied up. She kept her courage strong. She kept her secret well. Mulan became a famous officer and led her troops into many successful battles.

But every night she dreamed of her home, her mother, her father, and Little Brother. She wondered how they were.

Chapter 6

Finally the war was won. The emperor was pleased with Mulan.

"You have been brave and true," he said. "Ask for any reward, and you can have it. Gold? Diamonds? Palaces?"

25

Mulan knew exactly what she wanted.

"I want a fast horse, and I want my freedom!" she said. "I want to leave fighting behind and return to my family to live in peace."

Her wish was granted.

When Father and Mother heard the sound of horses' hooves, they came out to look. They saw a fine officer riding toward them.

It was Mulan, followed by her troop of soldiers. She looked so splendid, riding her fine horse.

Little Brother ran out to welcome the soldiers and to cheer.

Mulan went into the house to her old room. She sat at her table and took off her armor.

She let her hair down. She washed off the dust.

She put on her dresses, long and flowing.

Then she went outside and greeted her troop
of soldiers.

"I am Mulan," she said.

Her comrades were all amazed.

"A girl!" they shouted. "Not possible!"

It took a lot of explaining before they could
believe it.

The soldiers were so amazed that they told Mulan's tale far and wide. The story of how a young girl became a warrior spread from person to person. It crossed mountains and oceans to many different countries.

In Mulan's homeland people still sing about her.

It is hard to believe
that it could be so,
but now we have learned,
now we know
not to judge people
by how they look.
You, too, can be a hero
and have your tale told
or put in a book.

Once upon a time ...

The end.